Little Blue Truck Leads the Way

Written by

Alice Schertle

Illustrated by

Jill McElmurry

Harcourt Children's Books
Houghton Mifflin Harcourt
Boston New York

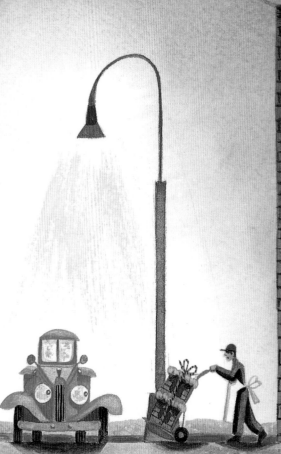

Harcourt Children's Books is an imprint of Houghton Mifflin Harcourt Publishing Company.
hmhbooks.com

The illustrations in this book were done in gouache on
Arches 140-lb. cold-pressed watercolor paper.
The text type was set in PT Barnum.
The display type was set in Rootin Tootin.

Library of Congress Cataloging-in-Publication Data
is available.
ISBN 978-0-15-206389-4

Printed in China
SCP 15 14 13 12 11
4500812314

For Kate and John, Jen and Drew, and those
two truckers Spence and Dylan. Beep! Beep!
—A.S.

For all my friends in New York City.
—J.M.

Horn went "**Beep!**"
Engine purred.
Friendliest sounds
you ever heard.

Little Blue Truck
rolled into the city.
"Beep! Beep! Beep!
Isn't it pretty?"

Towering buildings
scraped the sky.
"Beep!" said Blue.
"The city is *high!*"

"Shove on, Shorty!" yelled a double-decker bus with big red letters: RIDES-R-US.

A grocery truck
gave his horn a blast.
"MOVE IT, BUD—
I'M FIRST, YOU'RE LAST!"

Wooeeee...

went a siren.
"Coming through!
Busy police car,
things to do!"

SWISH! SWASH! SWOOSH!

went a big street sweeper,
hollering, "HEY!
BETTER MOVE, LITTLE BEEPER!"

"MAKE WAY!"
yelled a limousine
(the longest car
you've ever seen).

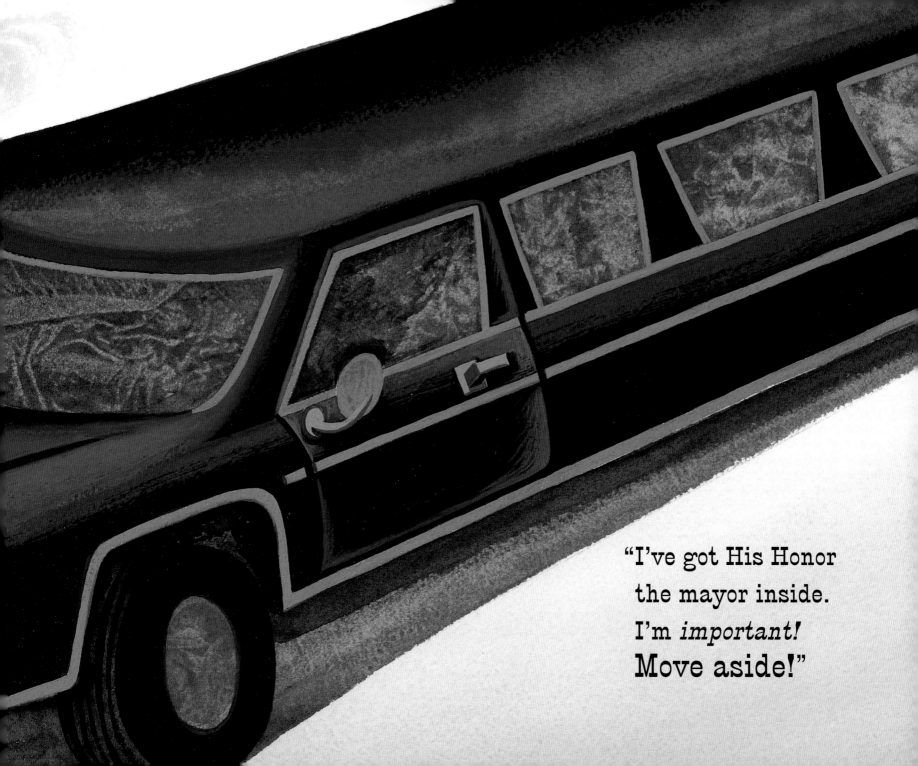

"I've got His Honor
the mayor inside.
I'm *important!*
Move aside!"

Cars and trucks
were all in a tangle.
Everyone started
to shout and wrangle.

Up roared a taxi.
Screech went the brakes.
"STOP!" yelled Blue.
"For goodness' sakes!

You might be fast
and I might be slow,
but one at a time
is the way to go."

"Me first!" said the limo,
all puffed with pride.
Then he gave a cough
and his engine died.

He was stuck right there
with the mayor inside.
"**Beep!**" said Blue.
"Would you like a ride?"

Everybody watching
gave a shout
when the door swung open
and the mayor stepped out.

His Honor climbed
right up on Blue
and gave a speech
(the way mayors do).

"My friends," he said,
"what wonderful luck—
this good advice
from a little blue truck!

One at a time
is what we'll do,
so single file, folks—
FOLLOW BLUE!"

Trucks and buses
got in line
with vans and taxis,
and it all went fine.

A taxi let
a van go past.
The double-decker bus
said, "I'll go last."

A marching band
joined the big parade.
BOOM! went the drums,
and the trumpets played.

They rolled along
the avenue
and everyone waved
to Little Blue.

Blue
is
Cool!

They clapped their hands and yelled, "HOORAY!" for the little blue truck who led the way.